A Change Of Views

Craig Anthony Hartley

A Change Of Views

GREECE, MOUNT OLYMPUS

From her pinnacle on Mount Olympus, Hera gazed out on her beloved domain. The view, once beautiful, did nothing to ignite her celestial being.

Having been used to hearing the voices of her Priestesses praying before her shrine, the sound of silence blanketed the landscape and she was saddened.

Her friends, Athena and Aphrodite, let her have this moment alone, so she could remember the former majesty of Greece. After what seemed like an eternity, she rejoined her comrades as they waited to be summoned by the Council to give voice to the inevitable truth.

Athena was still mouthing off about the whole affair.

"Do my people think that my shrine will still protect them from danger, even though they have forsaken us?"

"Our shrines and effigies are in England, not in Greece anymore." Hera wryly commented.

"I can't do with all this waiting, I prefer action to words. Let's confront the Council now."

"Curb your battle strategy for later."

Aphrodite chimed in. "Darlings, I've had this self same argument with my hubby. I hope they'll keep him overtime in the forge tonight." That got a laugh from both women.

The great white marble doors opened, while the women were talking and Hermes greeted them with a deep bow and a wink at Aphrodite. His gleaming white toga and golden sandals glowed by flickering torches from inside the Council Chambers.

"Ladies, the Council is ready to hear your dispute." Athena swept past, while Hera and Aphrodite glided.

The burnished golden thrones had been buffed earlier by satyrs, but they paled in comparison to the Weather God himself. Zeus commanded obedience.

Aphrodite broke the silence "I'll get straight to the point. The three of us," (she indicated her companions)" are disgusted by how Greece and the rest of the world have shaded their eyes against the true way."

"What is it that you suggest we do?" Zeus's voice rang through the chamber.

"Seek a different base than here. You already know they have shunned all ties to Olympus."

There was a collective gasp from all attendees. Hera stepped forward. "I concur with Aphrodite. Remember my usual role of interacting with mortals. They don't want my presence to be felt anymore."

Zeus interjected "Not surprising, remember a guy called Jason?" Hera flushed at the memory of the leader of the Argonaughts. (She had a schoolgirl crush on him and she had helped him on his famous journey by giving him solid advice).

Now she bristled at her husband's slur at her mortal cuddly boy.

"At least he accepted my advice, which right now is immaterial."

"Even I'm bored, gazing at the same old view. I crave adventure". Aphrodite continued.

"And more men," Hephaestus muttered under his sulphur smelling mouth, "I've finished my shift early." He explained to his wife.

She gave him a scornful look. "It is none of your business to interfere with my love life."

"Enough." Zeus bellowed.

Stability and calm flooded the chamber as Apollo spoke. "The goddesses have a point. They have aired their views and now await the Council's answer."

Zeus inclined his head towards Apollo in gratitude. "All those in favour of relocating?" The council as a body rose to their feet in acknowledgement.

"I feel like singing." Aphrodite told Hera afterwards.

"Don't let Apollo hear that, he'll start strumming the lyre."

Athena and Aphrodite laughed. They were sitting in Athena's white columned mansion, getting high on ambrosia and nectar until they heard faint music coming from a reedy pipe.

Aphrodite dashed over to the open window (she had tried to tempt a cool breeze in earlier), and heard a bleating laugh.

"I can't hear anyone singing."

"It was a figure of speech, Pan."

He chortled. "I'm just in high spirits about the move and I've got a suggestion where to relocate."

"Where?" Hera joined Aphrodite at the window.

"Pendle Hill in Lancashire, I've been there with Hermes on our travels. Plenty of sheep to hear my pipes and I have heard tell that frequently there's a mist over Pendle. We could easily hide our presences in it. Also, in addition, there are towns and villages to visit. I'm on my way to the Council Chambers to inform them of my idea."

"Pan, that's ideal," Athena came rushing over to join her companions at the window, "Why didn't I come up with that plan?"

After Pan had aired his views, Zeus pondered his answer. "It's got merit," he said at last, "instead of a mountain, we have to downsize. We are in a recession you know! Personally, I think it's ideal. I also like the idea of hiding in the mist."

"It's idyllic." Apollo said.

The rest of the Council nodded their heads in agreement and the vote was unanimous.

"I'm looking forward to the move." Hera said to her husband, later that night. Zeus accepted the proffered glass of ambrosia and nectar.

"I am, that was a clever decision of Pan's."

"When do we actually pack?"

"We don't, Apollo and I have thought it through and discussed it. It'll happen overnight."

"Really? How?"

"When we wake up, we automatically arrive in the mist over Pendle and our wardrobes will change into mortal clothes."

"We dress down?"

"Yes."

They both finished their drinks and went to bed.

Time eddied and flowed while the deities dreamed the dream of blissful slumber. The move to Pendle Hill had begun, the silver glow of the moon cast it's radiance into Aphrodite's bedroom and played upon her lithe features. She was definitely what the scribes had written about in ages past. Beauty personified in every detail.

She rolled over onto her side. Her brooch, shaped like a dove but with no back emblem, suddenly glowed purest bronze and the mystical light from the dressing table woke Aphrodite within a heartbeat.

She easily slipped out of bed without disturbing her husband and tiptoed over to inspect the source. As soon as she picked up her brooch, she cast her eye on her slumbering husband.

She felt no love for him anymore, she had truly given her heart to someone else and in so doing, had had his child. Then she heard it, a voice made manifest "What was divided is now made whole. A separation eons ago, now together again, never to part."

Aphrodite whispered in the darkness. "After all this time of searching, I will find my lost child again."

Apollo couldn't sleep, he tossed and turned while images danced around in his brain. The day he had to forego his pride and joy. His sister had assured him that her Huntresses would watch over and protect his son.

"You will find him again, when the time is right." The voice spoke in the wailing tone of his Oracle, but it wasn't his Oracle.

The shimmering flickering of Pendle Hill came into focus. A new day had dawned for the gods and goddesses of Olympus.

PENDLE HILL

As morning dawned, so did Hera. She cautiously peeped through the lace curtains and gasped in wonder.

Lush greenery overcast by grey clouds covered the landscape. It looked so drab, and yet more alive and fresher.

She dropped the curtain and went to get dressed. She threw open her wardrobe and got another shock. Jeans, blouses, strappy tops, combat trousers and miniskirts. She slammed the doors in disgust. The sound woke Zeus.

"What's up."

"When you said we had to dress down I didn't know you meant I had to wear these." She opened her wardrobe again and brandished a pair of jeans.

"What?"

Zeus jumped out of bed and opened his clothes cabinet. Jeans, t-shirts, combat trousers, long and short sleeved casual shirts and evening attire. "Cool," he commented.

"Where are my dresses?" Hera hurled at him.

"Don't get at me." He selected a deep blue short-sleeved casual shirt with eagle design and a matching pair of jeans. Resigned to the fact, Hera pulled out a white blouse and (in complete revulsion) a blue pair of jeans.

"Don't look at me, I'm hideous," she moaned once she got dressed.

"I am looking and you're beautiful," Zeus said in awe, "take a look in the mirror." Hera dejectedly gazed at her reflection and incredulity washed over her. She turned around, then back. She was completely in awe.

Suddenly the tranquil silence was rendered by a shriek and a curse. Zeus and Hera reacted as one as they burst through the door into bright sunlight. The sight that greeted them was lush greenery and an irate Aphrodite still in her night attire.

"What's the matter?" Hera asked.

"My wardrobe, that's what."

"Well, look at me."

Aphrodite looked. She took in Hera's garb and her jaw dropped.

"Wow," she breathed, "Picture this, slacks, strappy tops, *trousers*, and blouses. In my wardrobe."

"I know, same in mine."

Both goddesses glared at Zeus. "It's not my fault," he said in defence.

"Actually, you can blame me," Apollo wryly commented as he came out of his mansion and approached the agitated women. "I just thought it would be different and more modern, also, have you seen what Zeus and I have done to our mansions?"

They all turned to look, Zeus grinned at Apollo in acknowledgment. Pinewood log cabins were organised in a semicircle amongst the abundance of wildlife.

Aphrodite marvelled at the beauty. She immediately fell in love with the setting. Hera had a lump in her throat.

"We really have downsized, haven't we?" She asked Aphrodite.

"I may as well try to find something suitable to wear for these conditions." Aphrodite excused herself and hurried off. Hera and Zeus turned to Apollo. Zeus clapped the sun god's shoulder.

"You've done us proud, my friend."

Hera smiled fondly at her loyal supporter on the Council and for his wise and steadfast decisions, also coupled with his gentle humour, then she and Zeus went back to their cabin.

A couple of minutes later, Aphrodite walked in. She had changed into a blue denim miniskirt and a pale pink flowered blouse. Zeus's mouth was open in agog.

"So, you have found something to wear." That got a chuckle from the goddesses.

"Sulphur breath's missing the forge, so he's gone back to sleep." Aphrodite quipped while Hera roared with laughter.

Dressed in a black strappy vest, black combat trousers and military style boots, Athena felt feline and powerful. A lioness strutting her stuff.

She loved the scenery, and for the first time in eons, she felt *alive*. After scouting the foliage and admiring the view from Pendle, it was time to visit Hera.

She marched straight into Hera's cabin and created a stir. Zeus, Hera and Aphrodite's expression was amazement!

"Wow." Hera exclaimed.

"Let's swap attire." Aphrodite squealed.

"Shall we get hitched?" Zeus was amazed. Then, just to get some semblance of order, "Right, we are going to need a plan of action. Where do we go from here? We need a map of the towns and villages before we descend into the mortal world."

"The best person to help with that is Hermes, since he's the patron of travellers." Athena volunteered. She telepathically reached out to Hermes, who responded to her call.

He came a moment later, carrying a map which he spread out on a table.

"Right, this is a map of Great Britain. We are here, Pendle Hill. Some of the towns and villages in the area are Clitheroe, Skipton and Burnley. In addition, there are other places to visit

"Are there clothes shops?" Aphrodite asked.

"Yes, all the town in the area have what they call boutiques where they sell clothes, jewellery, ornaments and books. Other main attractions are Clitheroe Castle, Skipton is a historic market town and its castle is worth the visit. Also, if we want to sightsee other places, I can recommend Burnley, and it offers a music store, fashionable clothes stores, market hall and a stately home called Townley Hall."

Zeus and company were impressed. "There's something for everyone to peruse." The weather god said.

"I'm dying to visit a boutique." Aphrodite exclaimed.

"I'll come with you and we'll have a girls day out." Hera offered.

Zeus wasn't pleased. "What about my evening meal?"

"Make it yourself, it won't kill you." Hera bristled. Athena gave her the thumbs up.

"You know what; I'm starting to get hacked off with my hubby lounging around and missing his forge. I am going to give him the ire of my tongue." Aphrodite said as she flounced out of Hera's cabin. Everyone's jaw dropped open at her outburst.

Aphrodite had had enough with her husband, she was not going to be all sweetness and light. Hephaestus was going to get the full heat of his forge directed at him for a change.

She barged into her cabin, purposely nearly tore the door off its hinges as she marched into her bedchamber.

"Get out of that bed and do something useful." She virtually screeched.

"Oh, let me sleep." Hephaestus mumbled into his pillow. All of a sudden the sheets were yanked off.

"Get up now, we're on Pendle Hill." That got his attention.

"Sorry sweetheart, I thought we were still on Olympus," he yawned, "I'm getting up now, will you make me an ambrosia and nectar?"

"Make your own ambrosia. I've got things to do."

Once she was sure her husband was up and dressed, she met up with Hera and Athena. They dissipated into the mist materialised as mortals in Skipton.

SKIPTON

As they gazed in wonder at the strange sights and ignited by the babbling crowd, their eyes alighted on a familiar sight.

"A street market." Aphrodite squealed.

"Let's have a look." Hera said.

On one stall there were racks of clothes ready to peruse. "I wonder what we possess that we can barter with." Athena mused.

"That trading process was outdated years ago." A fair haired young man stepped forward from out of an alleyway. "I overheard your conversation."

Something above the women made him pause in mid conversation. A shimmering pulse of energy that seemed otherworldly, but laden with mortal matter radiated around them Athena noticed his dilemma and inclined her head.

"Yes, we are goddesses. I see there is no fooling you, young man. What's your name?"

"Anthony Kibble. Is that your natural auras made manifest to mortal standard?"

"You have a very perceptive intuition," Athena grinned, she instantly took a liking to Anthony, "you really are familiar with the old ways. I can tell. I'm with my friends, Aphrodite and Hera."

The two Goddesses came forwards as Athena introduced them. Hera asked him. "Are you local?"

"Yes, but I don't live around here. I come here frequently. I like to browse. There's a music stall just further up. I was going to have a look."

Hera fell into step with Anthony (while Athena and Aphrodite followed behind) Hera continued speaking. "Where else would you recommend visiting? We moved from Olympus to Pendle Hill."

Anthony's jaw nearly dropped. "Well, if you want to familiarise yourself with the local area, I can recommend Barrowford, which has a Heritage Centre and you can pick up tourist information leaflets."

"Just where is Barrowford?"

"If you like, I can take you in my car after we've finished browsing."

"What about my friends?"

"If they don't mind sitting in the back seat?"

Hera laughed. It had been eons since she had interacted with mortals. It felt good to be doing it again.

"Love to."

Anthony grinned. From reading Greek mythology, Hera was his all time favourite Goddess. He loved the stability, home and marriage he had been raised to believe in. He toyed with the idea of asking her out for tea, but didn't voice it.

Hera picked up on his wavelength. "Did you want to ask me something?"

"I was just playing with the idea of asking you out for a meal later tonight." He blushed.

"I would be honoured. Thank you." She smiled at him

As they neared the music stall, they heard Apollo's voice. All these songs are recorded onto a disk?"

"Welcome to the modern world, pal. Yes, this is called a CD, which you listen to on a CD player," explained the merchant.

"Apollo, it's us." Athena called.

"I'll be with you in a minute, just going to purchase this CD. Just where can you buy CD players from?"

"Any good electrical stores and supermarkets."

"What are supermarkets?" asked Athena as the goddesses and Anthony joined Apollo.

"Massive store complexes where they sell food produce, clothes, DVD's, DVD players, mobile phones and widescreen televisions. Also they have cafés where you can have a drink after you have finished shopping." Anthony piped in. The deities gaped in astonishment and wonder at the incredulity and the magnitude of a world they had never before encountered.

Apollo broke the moment, when he pulled out his wallet (the goddesses looked on in astonishment) and handed over the required price to the merchant.

After the purchase, Athena demanded "Where did you get that wallet and the money?"

"Part of the courtesy of the move. We now have modern currency."

"We haven't?"

Apollo waved his hand, each goddess had a shoulder bag. Apollo continued. "There's a purse inside that's bulging with money."

Aphrodite looked like she wanted to kiss him. Then Hera remembered Anthony. "Apollo, meet Anthony Kibble. Anthony, this is the god of music."

Anthony stepped forward. "Pleased to meet you, sir."

Apollo shook Anthony's hand

"Ages since we have interacted with mortals, you won't be the only one."

Anthony grinned. "I could fetch you up to speed on CD's DVD's and the current music of today. As a matter of fact, we could have a social drink sometime and talk about everything to do with entertainment."

"I would appreciate that, thanks."

"Burnley is the place to visit for music store and Clitheroe has a music shop which sells musical instruments."

"I think I'll check Burnley first."

"Also Burnley has boutique stores."

"Really?" Aphrodite's face looked like Christmas had come early. "I'm going to Burnley now that I've got proper money."

"May I have the honour of being your escort." Apollo asked her.

"This is just an excuse to browse that music store, but yes, kind sir." Apollo gave Anthony a conspiratorial wink. Anthony heard Apollo's voice inside his head.

"*I have been meaning to ask her out for eons.*"

Anthony grinned to himself knowingly.

"I wouldn't mind perusing the Heritage Centre." Athena remarked, "then meet up in Burnley."

"Anthony and I will stay in Skipton, we will have some lunch and then we'll come to Burnley," Hera informed her companions. Telepathically she told Aphrodite *"He's asked me out for a date and a meal later tonight."*

"He's fast. What are you going to wear?"

"That's why I need to peruse Burnley's boutiques."

Just for Anthony's amusement, Apollo put his arm around Aphrodite's waist and dissipated into the mist. The expression on her face was half repugnance and half-girly as she let him pull her along. Athena also vanished.

"Just us left," Anthony said to Hera. "There's a holistic fair in the Town Hall." They crossed over the road and entered the hall, Hera's face shone in awe and wonder as she observed mini stalls laden with crystals and jewellery. In addition, there were palmistry stalls and aura photography stalls and everything the eye could see.

"It's beautiful." She breathed. One of the shoppers looked straight at Hera. "Do you think my Huntresses would like these beads?" Artemis indicated the jewellery.

Hera introduced Anthony to Artemis, who instantly took a liking to him. Both goddesses browsed the bling and after they had finished, Anthony led the way towards an aura photography stall.

Hera and Artemis both looked interested. "I'm having mine taken." Anthony told them. He went over and the photographer led him to a chair and took his picture. After the photo had dried, Anthony saw red, gold and bronze colours over his head. He also received a print out of what the colours meant. Hera and Artemis gathered around to have a look.

"I've noticed a tea room. Shall we go and peruse this print out?" Artemis asked. Anthony and Hera agreed.

"According to the print out, gold is the highest of colours, but bronze is unknown." Artemis drained her tea. (The goddesses had ordered ambrosia and nectar earlier, but ended up being served tea instead.)

"Red goes to the base." Hera chimed. Seated two seats away, the god of war, Ares, listened to the conversation. The female deities knew he was present, but the mortal with them didn't. Ares knew who Anthony Kibble really was. Therefore, just to steer the conversation towards to what was virtually the truth, Ares materialized and joined in the chat.

"What about the make of our weapons, they're celestial bronze." The goddesses and Anthony all gaped in astonishment.

"Of course." Anthony breathed.

"You could be descended from the Ancient Greeks," laughed Hera. Ares came over to join them, as he approached, Anthony mentally heard. "*I know something that you don't, boy.*"

"Are you all right, Anthony, you've gone pale." Artemis reached over to take his hand.

"I think so." He swallowed hard. Just then, help came in the guise of a young child who looked completely lost.

"I can't find my mum."

Hera was first to her feet.

"It's all right, child. I'll help you find her."

"What's your last name?" Anthony asked kindly.

"Matthews." The boy said to Anthony and nodded his thanks to Hera. Anthony smiled to himself. Hera's title was patron of children, as well as for the home. The kid was in good hands.

Apollo was seething; he stared into the vacant music store and swore. Aphrodite walked up to him, carrying a boutiques store shopping bag.

"What's the matter?"

"A music store full of nothing," he snarled, "we should have gone to Clitheroe rather than Burnley." Aphrodite squeezed his arm in concern.

"We said we'll wait for Athena, Hera and Anthony. Come on, let's go to that café we saw earlier and sample a mortal drink."

Apollo's anger abated. "Sorry, honey," she melted into him. "I don't think Anthony knows about the store closure and us."

"We'll just tell him about the closure." Aphrodite smiled and led him up the street.

Anthony felt a wave of disappointment and anger wash over him, then it dissipated as soon as it came. The feeling that something had gone or had been closed down filtered through his thoughts.

Hera had managed to locate the child's mother and was busy chatting to her. Artemis closed her eyes for a moment then turned to Anthony.

"You felt the same emotions I've just experienced?"

"Yes."

"It's because he's my twin brother that I feel this connection," she smiled warmly, "somehow, we are also connected to each other."

Anthony suddenly remembered the book he had bought earlier, just before he had encountered the deities. "A Boy and a Dolphin." He fished it out of its bag and handed it over.

"I purchased this earlier and I haven't a clue why I was drawn to buy it."

Seeing Anthony and Artemis deep in conversation, Hera's face tightened. She did not want to see Anthony speaking to another woman, not even to another goddess. That thought rocked her. She was married to Zeus!

And here she was being jealous over a guy she had just met, "*who has asked me out later tonight for a meal*." She quickly returned her attention to Alice Matthews and her son, William.

"I know I've introduced myself as June, but my real name is Hera, Queen of Olympus." Alice's jaw dropped open.

"You mean June as in Juno. Goddess of ancient Rome?"

"Yes, that's how I was known, but I'm Greek in origin." (The Roman's adopted the Greek deities and gave them Roman names.)

William piped in. "I've always loved the tales of old. People write and document them. Even I read the books." Alice laughed.

"You better believe him, he's an expert on the subject." Hera's mouth quirked upward into a broad grin.

"All right then, William. Which son of Zeus thought that I was a wicked stepmother?"

"Easy, that was Hercules, also known as Heracles. Who was named after you." William's six year old face met the Queen's and he grinned.

Hera's heart went out towards Zeus for calling his offspring after her; she simply didn't realize just what degree of damage she had inflicted eons ago. Just because of her husband's philandering, she had become jealous. She didn't want her stepson to hate her for being a devoted housewife. She was just lonely and in love with her husband. Also she didn't want Zeus to look at another woman, let alone a mortal.

But, she realised, I'm doing the same with Anthony and getting my own back on Mr Stormy-face in the process. Go to it, girl.

Alice Matthews gently chastised her son. "I think you revealed too much."

"No," Hera shook herself out of her reverie, "you've got an intelligent young mind. We've moved from Olympus to Pendle Hill, and this young man," she indicated Anthony Kibble, "is our tour guide." Anthony made a face, which made the women laugh, and William gave him the thumbs up.

Hera gently smiled at William. "You will become a Professor of Greek Mythology; you have the passion and the love of the ancients."

She turned to Alice. "And you will come to know in due course that what I'm saying right now will come to pass and you will believe. Just watch and see what happens."

Both Alice and William's faces shone with awe and wonder, then the said their goodbyes and drifted back to mingle in the crowd once more.

All of a sudden, Athena was back in their midst. "I've found some literature from the Heritage Centre and I've browsed all over Barrowford. Aphrodite telepathically sent me a message. They are still waiting for us in Burnley, there's nothing for them to see and Apollo's miffed."

While Athena brought Hera up to date on what had transpired, Artemis continued her conversation with Anthony. "This brooch on the cover of your book is a dove of peace. There is only one goddess who symbolizes this emblem and when you arrive in Burnley, show this to Aphrodite. That's all I can tell you."

Ares (who had been privy to what had happened since William Matthews had encountered them) clapped Anthony on the shoulder,

"We immortals have tendencies to be aloof and set apart from ordinary people. Therefore, it is hard for me to swallow my pride and to ask if you could forget that I spooked you earlier." Anthony chortled and clapped Ares on the shoulder in return.

"No problem." Ares vanished just as Artemis asked if she could come to Burnley as well. The goddesses could dissipate into the mist, but, as a mortal, Anthony could not, so they all decided to take Anthony's car.

BURNLEY

When they pulled into Burnley's parking lot, they saw Aphrodite and Apollo waiting for them. Once Anthony parked up and the goddesses climbed out, Apollo exploded. "There's nothing worth seeing, no music store. Nothing."

"Let me tell them," Aphrodite soothed, "We've browsed all over. I've seen quite a few boutiques, but there's nothing for Apollo and as you can see, he's miffed."

"That's putting it mildly." Apollo muttered.

Anthony piped up. "There's a cracking book store in the centre. Why don't we have a browse there while the ladies go shopping?"

Apollo sagged with relief. "I appreciate that. Thanks."

Once the men sauntered towards the centre, Hera saw herself back on Mount Olympus, gazing down on the meandering snake of slivery grey rivers and seas that once were blue. Everything was hushed and heavy, no voice of her priestesses praying before her shrine. The people had rejected the deities. They felt useless and unwanted.

Then she heard a voice saying "Now is the time of the modern woman, they are not shackled by their men. Look around you, observe their attire and their ways."

Then all of the goddesses felt a great swelling and stirring engulf them. Hera felt like she wanted nothing better than to ditch Zeus and have a fling with Anthony. They all felt an empathy with the modern woman.

The voice they had just heard was the call of modern times. All the goddesses of Mount Olympus had been freed.

Aphrodite whooped (which she never would have dared before) "I want to see *everything* now. We are liberated goddesses. " The women burst out into peals of laughter.

Artemis (who was always the organizer, goddess of the hunt, twin sister of Apollo and trainer of young girls) shouted.

"Vote for women! When I get back to Pendle Hill I'm going to arrange and set up a campaign for us goddesses to be treated as equals by our men."

She strode towards Burnley centre, leaving the rest following in her wake. "Hurry it up, slowpokes!" she called over her shoulder.

"Artemis, slow down," Hera panted.

"I can't gear down," Artemis called back. (Of all the goddesses to quickly modernize, Artemis, Aphrodite and Athena were the first ones).

A hardcore teenage girl with shoulder length red flaming hair strode past and gave Artemis a calculating look.

"Hey Art. Adapted to the new life yet?"

"Getting there, Ruby Cameron." Artemis slowed her pace.

"You know I prefer to be called Red, don't you?"

"As you keep reminding me."

When Artemis slowed, the rest of the goddesses caught up.

"This is why I was in a rush. Everyone, this is Ruby Cameron. My head Huntress, who prefers to be called Red."

Hera nodded at Ruby. "We were on our way for me to buy a new dress for my date with a young man called Anthony Kibble."

Ruby's mouth fell open at the mention of Anthony's name. Anthony Kibble was a hero to the Huntresses. Someone they aspired to. She quickly closed her mouth before anyone had noticed.

"To tell you the truth," Hera told her friends, "I'm not really bothered about the date. I need to explain this to Anthony."

"I will." Ruby said, "Where is he?"

"He's gone off with Apollo towards the centre." Hera smiled inwardly to herself. She had seen Ruby's reaction towards Anthony's name. It wasn't fair to the young girl to deny her the right to meet and train the legend that the Huntresses held in high esteem.

As she strode into Burnley centre, Ruby's face turned the same colour as her hair. "Stop it!" she ordered herself. Since the goddesses had thrown of the shackles of bondage, so had the Huntresses.

But Ruby still found it hard not to blush when Anthony's name was mentioned. She was nowhere near the same age as her hero, but she was a dreamer. She fancied herself in his arms.

"And then I spied this book," Anthony flourished at Apollo, "A Boy and a Dolphin." Apollo took the book from Anthony and peered closely at it, "also this brooch, Artemis told me it was a dove."

They were having a health drink in a jazz café. Apollo ruefully smiled.

"My sister hasn't got the gift of prophecy as I have, but she is right in essentials. The symbol is a dove. The symbol that represents me is a laurel tree."

It's just a story, nothing more. If you need proof, then I suggest you look more closely at this holistic picture".

Anthony looked once again at his depicted aura, the bronze colouration caught his eye. Apollo nodded.

"Did Ares tell you in Skipton that the colour of our weapons are celestial bronze?"

"Yes, inside the Town Hall café."

"Before you met Alice and William Matthews?"

"Yes."

Apollo's face sparkled like the rising sun, and for a brief moment, Anthony felt awed to be in the presence of the sun god.

"Anthony. Aphrodite and I had a child who was taken from us eons ago. My sister's Huntresses allied themselves to be his protectors and personal instructors. He was struck down in his prime, but now, eons later. He has been re-born."

Apollo's voice broke with emotion for the first time as he gazed at Anthony. Anthony stayed stock still, mentally weighing what he was hearing and it all made undeniable sense.

The bronze in his aura was because he was an Olympian. His home was Mount Olympus and he was pure god. Not a demigod like the legendary heroes of old.

"All this time, it was a set up to find me?"

"The move to Pendle Hill was our idea. Only one god doesn't know your true heritage. Hades, Lord of the Underworld. Also he thinks that you're an usurper to take command of the Huntresses, because, in his opinion, you are a mortal man. He'll try to thwart you at any cost".

"I thought your sister's in charge of the Huntresses?"

"She is, but times have changed, she wants to hand over the reins to you since she's your aunt. Also," Apollo trailed off when a redheaded teenage girl strode in the café, spotted both men and walked over.

"Hey Red," Apollo acknowledged her, "Anthony, this is Ruby Cameron, who prefers to be called Red. Ruby, meet Anthony Kibble."

Ruby's heart fluttered in her chest. *"He's so handsome with his brown hair and eyes. I bet his arms are warm and strong."*

"I've just come to deliver a message from Hera." She damped down the impulse to blush when Anthony smiled.

"She's broken off the date," he replied.

Apollo silently sent Anthony the last part of their earlier conversation.

"Also it is the dawning of your time, for you will lead the Huntresses and you will be trained by Ruby Cameron, who is your aunt's head Huntress."

Anthony scrutinized Ruby, he liked what he saw and grinned. Both men downed the last gulps of their drinks; Ruby led them out to the street and virtually ran into Aphrodite and Ares.

As soon as Anthony opened his palm, she saw the other half of her brooch and she also saw the radiant expression on Apollo's face, Aphrodite's heart soared. She grabbed Anthony and held him tight.

"My son." She held him for what seemed to be an eternity. Mother and son separated, now always together.

Even Ares, the god of war, was touched.

"I was right about your aura and our celestial weapons being the same colour."

Aphrodite broke the embrace first, Anthony clasped Ares' hand.

"You sure were."

"Would you like to see how they are made inside Hephaestus's Forge?"

"I'll take him." Aphrodite volunteered. Ares nodded and dissipated into the mist.

"He's gone back to Pendle Hill." Aphrodite said at Anthony's expression.

"How am I going to get to the forge?" Anthony asked his mother.

"Let me carry and place you there. Close your eyes and put your trust in me."

Anthony did what he was told. Huge immortal hands, ever so gentle, cradled and softly placed him in front of the forge.

"That smells vile." Anthony retched as his nose detected sulphurous fumes. He opened his eyes. A mountainous crater spewing lava met his vision, and Ruby Cameron holding her nose in disgust. Ruby raised her voice to be heard over the eruptions under the earth.

"If you look up and to the right, you'll see Mount Olympus."

Anthony craned his neck and gazed in wonderment at the jewelled bronze gates towering slightly above him, silhouetting the entrance to the home of the immortals. Aphrodite squeezed his shoulder.

"When the time is right and your material work is done. You will join us, my son."

Aphrodite led the way down the treacherous strewn terrain towards the very heart of the crater. Here, the fumes nearly engulfed Anthony and Ruby. Only Aphrodite wasn't affected.

She stopped at a rusted iron door that was left open and a note left on it saying *"You forgot to lock up, dummy. Aphrodite."* Ruby smothered a laugh as the trio walked straight through into enveloping darkness.

A faint subdued light illuminated the pathway ahead, dimly lit torches glowed within their brackets. Ruby stayed close to Anthony for comfort. This part she didn't like. The smell of sulphur got worse as they approached another iron door.

Bronze statues of the deities flanked either side as Ruby stepped forward for the first time and knocked. Anthony looked perplexed until a voice came floating through the door beyond.

"Is that you, Red?"

"Yes, Sofia. Let us in."

The door softly glided open to reveal a Grecian beauty, her dark hair shone and her sapphire eyes sparkled as she ushered them inside. Anthony's jaw nearly fell open. The teenage beauty batted her eyelashes in mock flirtation and grinned.

Ruby's jaw tightened at her lieutenant's display towards Anthony, then ignored it.

Sofia closed the door behind them and turned to face her commander. Anthony's eyes alighted on a table filled with medallions and old Greek drachma. While Ruby and Sofia conferred, Aphrodite ushered Anthony towards the laden table.

She picked up a medallion with the emblem of the dove and the laurel tree. "This was left here eons ago by your father and I." Anthony automatically put it around his neck. As soon as metal met flesh he saw the antechamber in its former glory. Everything was pulsing with vibrant energy, coins, jewels and encrusted swords glowed in their grandeur.

"Yes, you can see through the eyes of the immortals now, what was once viewed as ruins to mortal eyes are alive to us. Follow Ruby, she will lead you to the Parthenon. There you will be trained to harness your immortal powers and hunter skills. I must return to Pendle Hill." Aphrodite smiled fondly at her son just as Ruby approached. Aphrodite dissipated.

"Sofia's gone ahead to the Parthenon and she will meet us there. Your true life starts now." Ruby took his hand and guided him down a side passage that led away from the antechamber.

REALM OF HADES

Deep in the bowels of the Underworld, Hades silently pondered what his agent had disclosed. Anthony Kibble, that mortal upstart, had been located by the gods and had dared to become leader of the so-called Huntresses.

Hades had always monitored whoever was conceived, raised to adulthood and died. An endless cycle of which he was Lord and Master. Whereas his brother Zeus was quick tempered, he was coldly calculating.

Therefore, he sat on his obsidian skull like throne and thought about how to discredit Anthony Kibble in the eyes of the Olympian gods.

A wail of despair echoed from the river Styx that ran through the Underworld. "Hera, Queen of the Gods. Why have you left us in our direst need? Our once proud nation has fallen into chaos and we are forced to endure hard times. Please answer us."

Hades had blanketed and smothered the voices of the various Priestesses of the gods so that they would think that they weren't needed anymore. Only Hades himself hadn't broken with the old ways, but Zeus's lot had left Olympus undefended and became modern.

There was only one person he had fed images of the epoch to chronicle the history of the gods, Homer. How fitting it would be to restore him from the Underworld and to waylay Anthony by his ramblings. (Homer was the first of many Greek authors who wrote Greek mythology around 750 BC. His literary works consist of "The Iliad", written about the Trojan War and "The Odyssey" written about the adventures of Odysseus. He is also known for his poetry).

Hades rose from his throne, stretched forth his gnarled hand towards the river Styx and commanded

"Homer, come forth. Your time is not yet over." His voice was ice cold with a touch of black humour. There was an answering breath of stale air and a shimmer in the hallowed waters. A breeze stirred to form eddies that lapped against crumbling rock, a whirlpool emerged to reveal an ancient white beaded man whose craggy features were dripping with droplets of water. After the droplets had vanished, the skin had become whole and new. Dexterity and sinew propelled Homer onto dry land and into middle age.

His eyes sparkled with gentle amusement and his voice was a gentle baritone. "Hades, I only serve to foretell the myths, not to use them for your own gratifications."

"I need your assistance, find a young man called Anthony Kibble, who is now inside The Sanctuary of Healing and use your ramblings to distract him from his objectives."

"That being?"

"None of your business. Just do what I command, or I will send you back to the Underworld to rot."

"I haven't got much choice. Alright, I'll do it."

"Just make sure you are clothed first." Homer smirked as he peered at his torso.

PENDLE HILL

Artemis was silently fuming at her brother, he was moping around and not behaving like his radiant self. All because there was no connection with the modern world regarding his music and his love of the arts.

Finally, she snapped at him. "Do something about it."

"Like what?" he mumbled.

"Get with the times, modernise yourself. I'm sure the modern world doesn't strum the lyre anymore. Get another instrument. As a matter of fact, here's some money," she virtually threw her purse at him. "Check out that music shop at Clitheroe that Anthony told you about. And don't come back until you made a purchase." Apollo looked dumbfounded at his sister. "Go now." She barked.

He ran for it, chagrined to be chased off by his twin sister and the indignity of carrying a purse. She mentally projected a vision of his lyre smashed beyond repair, so he had to buy a new instrument.

"He was just moping around and I saw red." Artemis explained to Hera just as Aphrodite and Athena joined them. They were sitting in Artemis's cabin, discussing Apollo.

"He needed a wakeup call." Athena commented.

"Honey, you did the right thing." Aphrodite's voice dripped with sugary sweetness and sarcasm.

Artemis looked at Hera for advice. "You're the organizer, not me, set up an event to bring music back into your brother's life. I know what he's going through. I felt the same way when my Priestesses stopped praying before my shrine and I couldn't connect to the modern world. He feels his music has gone and he can't function without it. He needs a purpose, not a sister that smashes his lyre and blows up in his face."

Artemis blanched. "I guess I overreacted."

"Where are the pieces now?"

"In the bin."

Hera rose to her feet, retrieved the pieces of the lyre and reformed the instrument into a mandolin. "Which is more in keeping with the times." She said to Artemis.

After her friends had left, Artemis mulled over what Hera had said.

She didn't know her brother felt broken and raw inside, ever since the goddesses had become modern, Artemis had severed the twin bond with her brother.

That is what modern women did these days, consider themselves as being equal to their men and Artemis was sickened by it. So was Hera. Only Aphrodite and Athena enjoyed every aspect.

Idly, she picked up the transformed lyre-turned-mandolin and felt an overwhelming urge to create a event to showcase her brother's talents and also to broadcast to every mortal that the gods and goddesses of Mount Olympus were residing on Pendle Hill. An all new site for people to pay homage and acknowledge the deities, as they once did.

The door to the cabin opened and Apollo sidled in, looking sheepish. "I couldn't find another instrument. I've looked all over."

Artemis turned to look at him, saw his dejected expression and the sisterly love flooded back. "Forgive m..."

Before she could say "me." Apollo walked over and opened his arms, she pulled him into a bear hug.

"Hera told me what you were going through."

"She's one smart woman." Apollo's eyes fell on the mandolin and his mouth literately fell open. "Where did you get that?"

"Your old lyre, Hera transformed it."

As soon as god and instrument made physical contact, images of music festivals, live concerts through the ages and up to modern day pop standards flashed through Apollo's mind. The call of modern times spoke "Entertainment and the arts have evolved. Rock it, man and get gigging."

The sound of a harmonica floated through the cabin's window and Pan waved at brother and sister. "Look what I've just bought." He shouted joyfully.

Apollo shouted back "Hey man, do you want to jam?" Artemis was amazed. She had never heard her brother speak in modern terms before.

"Why not. Yeah." Pan bounded through the cabin door. Apollo thought hard about which tune to play.

"Do you remember that jaunty ditty you did for King Midas in the old days?" Pan asked.

"When Dionysus and I had that bogus competition?"

"When you gave the king donkey's ears."

Apollo guffawed with laughter at the memory. "Yeah, well, I was a sore loser." The different chords from the mandolin felt natural to the sun god's fingers as he and Pan began to play. Artemis hummed the tune under her breath, not really paying much attention until Apollo stopped playing and looked at her in astonishment.

"What?" She asked

"When did you learn to sing like that?" He demanded.

"I didn't sing."

"You did, sis. Perfect pitch as well. Let's do it from the top." He started to play again while his sister sang. Unbeknown to the trio, Hera, Athena and Aphrodite were listening in from outside, until the heavens opened and snow descended with a cold wind factor.

Aphrodite hammered on Artemis's cabin door. "Let me in, quick. I'm getting snow in my hair." The music kept on playing amid girlish laughter, which was definitely not like Artemis at all. Even Hera had to hide a grin; she knew that Artemis was rubbing it in Aphrodite's and Athena's noses for being modern. She decided to play along as well.

"They haven't finished jamming just yet." Hera explained. Athena glared. "I wish there was enough snow to make a snowball."

Aphrodite continued to pound on the door while Hera said coolly

"So you could throw it in my direction."

Both Goddesses faced off against one another, just at the same moment Artemis opened the door. Aphrodite dashed inside, her hand itching to smack someone's face.

Athena and Hera followed suit, still glaring at one another. Apollo was quick to notice the subtle change in the women's auras, but wisely kept his own council. Aphrodite brushed snowflakes out of her hair and she let them fall on Artemis's floor. Apollo and Pan quickly excused themselves and dashed out of the cabin into the comforting sleeting snow.

"I wonder what's got into them?" Pan exhaled in relief.

"It's just what modern women do in a confrontation. Let them squabble, they will find out that modern ways are not always the right ways," Apollo said sagely.

"Too true." Zeus appeared wearing an all weather outdoor jacket that was zipped up to the neck and a pair of thick gloves.

"I never predicted this sort of weather."

"It all depends on the weather inside my sister's cabin." Just as Apollo said that, a rock hard snowball came in his direction, he ducked and Zeus caught the mound of snow flush in the face.

"Ow."

Pan burst out laughing and once Apollo stood back up he started to guffaw.

"You think it's funny?" Zeus bent down and gathered a handful of snow.

"Yes, we do." Apollo and Pan scooped up more snow.

"It's just like men to start a war." Hera's voice floated from Artemis's cabin, her voice cut through the girlish laughter.

"Right," Zeus locked eyes with Satyr and the sun god, "open the cabin door and let's have snow ammo."

"You wouldn't dare, ok girls, start making snowballs."

Hera was enjoying herself. She had plastered Athena with a snowball off the cabin's windowsill and Artemis had showered Aphrodite with a handful of cold snow. The goddesses had become friends again.

Now they were ready to take the fight to their men for keeping their wives under their thumbs all these eons.

PARTHENON

Ruby Cameron set up ten coke cans on top of the highest wooden beam, and then shimmied down the ladder she had erected earlier to join Anthony. He had already perfected the bow and arrow and had bested Sofia at their last bout of archery.

His last archery opponent was Ruby and he was looking forward to the competition. Now, he had progressed to firearms. He hefted his Smith and Weston, aimed at the first coke can and squeezed the trigger. The can shattered. Methodically, he inched the barrel over to the next target. That one also shattered. He slowly finished off the rest.

"You need to be a lot quicker than that." Ruby said as Sofia climbed the ladder and set up more cans.

Once they were aligned, Ruby stepped up, aimed and blasted all ten in one swift movement. Anthony looked crestfallen.

"Your turn to set them up, Anthony," Sofia trilled.

"You're just my second in command, Sofia. While I'm present, I issue orders." Ruby's voice turned cold and commanding. Even her hand was itching to slap Sofia's face.

Ruby turned to Anthony. "You're doing fine, it'll come." (Under her breath, so only Anthony could hear, she said, "It would be best to set them up. I'll put her on patrol duty, she doesn't like that.")

Anthony nodded, then climbed the ladder. Emptied ten more cans out of the crates and laid them on display. Just for Ruby's benefit, he grabbed hold of the sides of the ladder and let gravity slide him down. Both girls' hearts went aflutter.

Sofia muttered, "Show off." Ruby was inwardly impressed. Just one more round of firearm training, then back to the barracks for R and R.

Anthony stepped up, gun aimed dead centre and he fired ten times more rapidly than Ruby. All ten cans exploded. Ruby was amazed and fizzing at the same time.

"Right, Sofia, set them up for me. Increase amount to twenty. Watch this, Anthony Kibble." Sofia did what was requested. Ruby waited until the cans were lined up, and then she let rip with her weapon. All twenty were demolished.

"Try to beat that, Anthony."

"Stack them up again, Sofia. Make it thirty." Sofia did so, grinning at Anthony's attitude. Anthony hardly looked, just cleared all thirty cans into rubble. Turned to Ruby and shrugged.

"Try to beat that, Ms Ruby Cameron." Both girls' burst into peals of laughter, and Anthony joined in.

Ruby downed a coke and then stashed the can into a crate, so it could be used for target practise. She was in the middle of relax and recreation, when Anthony entered.

She tossed him a coke, which he opened and downed in one, threw it back and she tossed it in the crate to join its brother.

"I'm supposed to be training you, not to be shown up."

"Still stinging from target practise earlier? I had to make sure I got my eye in first." She relented. Her tough demeanour was just a cover. She was drilled to make Anthony toughen up, then to open him up to harness his immortal powers.

"I think I've got it. Hera broke off the date because you've got a crush on me."

Ruby smiled and nodded. "Sorry Anthony."

"Don't be." He had already assessed the situation and he knew what his response would be. He surprised her by pulling her into a warm embrace. She melted into his arms, inwardly purring.

"I'm too old; I'm in my 30's." He softly murmured against her ear.

"I know, I'm too young as well. I really like you though."

Anthony gently laughed.

"Hey, I just need to toughen up and be efficient in combat situations before I train to be immortal."

"I'll help you there, buster." They parted.

"What's on the agenda for tomorrow?"

"Our archery competition. Remember?"

"Oh, yeah. I forgot." She punched him. Sofia's voice came over the loudspeakers.

"I think we got trouble topside. There's a middle aged man staggering towards the Sanctuary. What shall I do?"

Ruby asked. "Is he an immediate threat?"

"No weapons detected. Just staggering."

Anthony quickly assessed the situation again. He made his choice.

"Ruby, power up the weapon emplacements. I'll wait at the entrance and if he's not any threat whatsoever I'll give you a hand signal to power down."

Ruby was awestruck at Anthony's sound tactics and manner.

"Did you copy that, Sofia?" She asked. Sofia double clicked the loudspeakers in confirmation and whistled.

Anthony marched to the entrance and down the steps. The complex's weapons came to bear. Outside, the sun burnt his back. "So this is what it's like through the eyes of the immortals", thought Anthony. "I wonder if Greece is to a mortal, subdued in comparison to this."

The man staggered forward and collapsed into Anthony's arms.

"I'm unarmed and not as supple as I used to be. You might not believe me, but I'm Homer." The man's face looked haggard and drawn. Anthony made a hands down gesture and the weapons retracted.

Moments later, Ruby arrived and helped to pry the man away from Anthony. "He said he's called Homer." Anthony explained.

"He can't be. Homer was a Greek writer ages ago. This guy's younger than that."

"I was resurrected by Hades, young lady; he wants me to find a young man called Anthony, to waylay him by my ramblings. Hades thinks I'm senile. I only said I would so I could get away. That's my only defence."

"Get him inside, Ruby." Anthony commanded. Somehow, he had found his inner strength. Ruby picked up on his overall manner.

"Yes sir."

She helped to prop Homer to his feet and led him into the Sanctuary. Anthony stayed outside, thinking about what had transpired. He felt hunted. His father, Apollo, had told him about Hades and how he had planned to use his minions to stop Anthony at all cost.

Suddenly Greece looked dark and foreboding, like it did to the legendary heroes. Nothing changes, what goes around, comes around.

Anthony couldn't sleep that night, he couldn't stop seeing a menacing, cruel visage in his dreams. Suddenly, he sat up in bed, cold sweat trickling down his face.

The room was dark and cool, he tremulously threw back the covers and extracted himself from the sheets. He let the coolness calm him, as he paced the floor. He needed a plan, he needed to accelerate his immortal training and for that he needed Ruby Cameron.

"Ruby." Anthony whispered urgently to her sleeping form. She woke with a start, then saw Anthony's face.

"What is it." She whispered back. Anthony filled her in about everything that had happened to him.

"I need to open myself up to harness my spiritual gifts. It's the only way I can be assured of being protected, and I'm scared."

"I'll help you." She completely forgot about the age difference and she pulled him to her. He let her do it and she just held him until the morning came.

PENDLE HILL

"I can't sing to save my life." Aphrodite said, aghast.

"You are an immortal." Athena quipped. Hera laughed at the pun. Artemis had the idea of setting up a music festival and she wondered if her friends would be interested to participate. Hera and Athena were all for it.

"I know some songs, but to perform them on stage with people watching." Hera shuddered at the thought.

"Wouldn't bother me, but I only know just one." Athena mused. She suddenly turned tearful.

"What is it?" Hera asked.

"It just reminds me of Greece," Athena brushed the tears away. "The White Rose of Athens." She sobbed harder. The other goddesses felt it then, an overwhelming emotional pull to go back home.

"We have to stay until we've had the music festival, so that people will come to honour and pray to us again. This is why we moved from Mount Olympus, to set up a new base of operations for us to be acknowledged again. If people know we're in their midst again, they will come to pay homage once more," Artemis explained.

Her friends looked at her and inclined their heads in acceptance and for her well reasoned plan.

"All right, we're going to have to form a band. Who do we know, apart from Apollo, who plays musical instruments?" Hera asked.

"There's Pan." Artemis said.

Aphrodite recovered her composure. "I could try to sing. People will love my presence on stage." She parted her new skirt with silts up the sides and revealed some leg.

"Hey boys, are you ready to rock?" She said in a bluesy husky voice.

Artemis, Hera and Athena literally gaped in astonishment.

"You're a natural." Artemis exclaimed.

"And also we can form a quartet." Aphrodite continued.

All the goddesses were fired up now and said "Why not." all at once.

Later, in her cabin, Hera told Zeus about Artemis's idea. "I've always wanted to play the drums," he commented.

"I never knew that! I better brush up my skills on the piano again."

Hera's fingers caressed the ivories of her Steinway, she summoned her songbook and sat down on the piano stool. She flicked through the pages and found a likely number for the band, "Blues in the Night". Her fingers glided over the keys until she heard her cabin door open and Aphrodite's voice came floating through, singing the words, in an husky tone.

"I'm in the living room," Hera called. Aphrodite walked through, still singing, her voice getting stronger and more powerful every minute.

Hera was amazed at the hidden potential within Aphrodite, she was a born singer!

"Have you got anymore songs lined up for me?" Aphrodite asked as she entered Hera's living room.

Hera laughed. "I think so, let's have a look together." The goddesses perused the songbook, pausing over some likely numbers they could use.

"That one looks possible for the quartet." Aphrodite mused. Hera looked at the title, "Super Trooper". Her fingers danced over the piano keys again and sang along with Aphrodite. Occasionally using some hip movement. They flicked through the sheet music for a good two hours, singing along to some of them. It felt good and different to Hera to liven up and Aphrodite to gel more in common with the home and the housewife. Over the eons they had clashed, but now they had mellowed and to bounce off one another verbally.

In Artemis's cabin, Athena and the goddess of the hunt also started to gel. They had collared Apollo earlier about getting a band together and he was ecstatic and eager, but only if Pan and Zeus were available. By telepathically speaking to Hera, they had assured him that Zeus wanted to play the drums and that Hera was going to play the piano.

Athena consented to play the bass and Apollo collared Pan, later that day, who was over the moon. Thus, the Band of the Immortals was born.

PARTHENON

Homer observed Anthony, he felt pity for the young man, he knew Anthony didn't trust him anymore than the two girls did. He wanted to apologise and to prove that he was indeed who he said he was.

"Curse you, Hades," he thought bitterly. Then it came to him, Hades had fed him images of the epoch for him to chronicle. The stories and the myths of the gods!

Anthony snapped out of his semi trance (the first part of opening himself was to break the earthly shell). Ruby Cameron monitored his progress.

"Anthony," Homer quietly spoke. "Ask me any question on Greek Mythology."

"Who was the trainer of heroes?" Anthony's voice was oddly subdued.

"Chiron the Centaur." Homer also kept his voice like Anthony's. Anthony thought long and hard, then finally asked.

"Which mortal man had an a affair with Aphrodite?" Everything seemed to hang on Homer's answer. Anthony knew what Homer was trying to do. He wanted Anthony to trust him, if he answered correctly, Anthony would believe him to be sincere.

"Adonis," Homer replied.

Anthony walked over and held out his hand in apology.

"I had to make certain. I'm sorry we've been hostile."

"You don't know how much of a hold Hades had over me. Aphrodite's your mother, isn't she? That's why you asked that particular question."

"Yes she is."

"Let me help you with your immortal training, I can teach you the ways of the old heroes and how they lived and worshiped the gods."

Anthony clasped Homer's hand in gratitude and in so doing he saw William Matthews staring back at him, Anthony suddenly became aware that Homer had been reborn, and he had actually met him earlier with Hera in Skipton.

No wonder Hera had said to William that he would someday become a world renowned Professor of Greek Mythology and that he had the love of the ancients. Anthony could see that now.

Homer softly said, "Chiron was the best trainer the ancient world had ever known. He trained men such as Hercules and Achilles, and his skills were legendary."

Anthony felt a stirring that seemed to echo from the ages past, calling to him as he listened to Homer's voice. Even Ruby and Sofia listened with curiosity.

A breeze sprang up and it seemed to quiet Anthony's fears, his eyes drooped, Homer's voice drifted in and out, and the earthly shell finally broke.

Sofia and Ruby gasped in wonder as Anthony glowed with pure golden light and he grew to block out the heavens themselves. Both girls looked at one another, then, they too, joined Anthony as pure energy themselves.

"You've done it, Anthony." Ruby's voice vibrated.

Anthony opened his eyes and held up his hands. They glowed luminescent and he gasped in wonderment and awe.

"Wow." He breathed, his voice thrummed like Ruby's. He heard Homer's distant voice.

"Thank you for trusting me, Anthony Kibble. You are truly the Son of Apollo and Aphrodite. I need to disappear because my time is over now. I was resurrected by Hades, now I need to return to be vapour once again. Goodbye my friend." Everything fell silent and hushed.

Only Anthony, Ruby and Sofia hung in the infinite silence. Ruby came towards Anthony.

"It is time to come and meet the Huntresses. Just think where you want to go and your thoughts will take you there." Anthony concentrated on finding the Huntresses and he dissipated into the mist.

THE WILDFORESTS OF GREECE

Girlish laughter assailed Anthony's ears, he opened his eyes and he was back to being mortal.

"No, you are not mortal anymore, you can move place to place just by thought alone. You only project the image of being mortal and have mortal perceptions as you once had." Ruby's voice was lighter and chirpy.

Anthony looked to his left and found her standing next to him. She punched him in the arm.

"Can you feel that?"

"Yes, ouch."

"When next you think of a place to visit, you'll dissipate again."

"So, that's how it works." She made to punch him again.

"All right, I'll believe you."

Sofia came over to meet them with about 15 other girls. All of them had the same hardened expression as Ruby and wore green military trousers and combat shirts.

They also carried assault rifles slung over their backs and had a banner depicting Artemis on the hunt. They saluted Ruby in crisp unison and ogled Anthony. One huntress battered her eyelashes at him.

"Everyone, this is Anthony Kibble," Ruby addressed her troops. One of them swooned at Anthony's name. All the girls laughed. Ruby smothered a grin. "Anthony is going to stay with us. He has received training with Sofia and I at the Parthenon, and now it's down to all of you to show him the ropes."

One of the girls came forward and introduced herself directly to Anthony. "Welcome to our camp, I'm Mia." She had shoulder length velvet black hair and a scar disfigured her jaw line, which stood out in plain sight.

She hooked her arm through Anthony's and led him briskly towards the Huntresses encampment. Ruby's jaw clenched as one by one, the rest of the troop followed suit.

Sofia met Ruby's eye. Both girls were resolute to keep Anthony for themselves.

PENDLE HILL

Hera had the best band practice she had ever had. The Band of the Immortals was coming along very nicely. Aphrodite's voice was getting better and better with each session.

She was sitting outside her cabin, enjoying the lush greenery and welcoming the sun's hot rays when she heard a strong vibrant voice emitting from the mortal world.

"Help me. I'm lost. Help." The sender sounded like a child. Hera closed her eyes and mentally asked for aid to go out, then she felt that a mother had finally responded to the ethereal touch and had found her child.

Suddenly, Pendle Hill raised itself and became slightly greener than usual. Hera felt the transition, as did Athena and Aphrodite as they came over from their cabins.

"We're needed once again; someone has called out for aid." Athena commented.

"Why has the hill grown?" Aphrodite wondered aloud.

"I have never been visited by the gods and goddesses of old before. Each positive thought and deed lifts me higher and higher until I become like your Mount Olympus. A new focal point since you arrived." The hill responded.

The goddesses looked at each other in awe and wonder. Out of the shrubbery stepped a nymph. His greenish skin looked exactly like the colouration of the hill, his pebble like eyes peered up at the goddesses.

"You awakened me at long last. I once was dormant, but now I am alive. I'm the nymph of the hill, my ladies." He squeaked.

Aphrodite fell in love with him completely. "You're adorable." She cooed.

He blinked his eyes and shyly winked. She tinkled with laughter. Hera and Athena marvelled at the sight of the hill nymph.

Zeus hurried over. "I've just been listening to the reports in the mortal world. All their canals, lakes and reservoirs are turning deep vivid blue and pure. Also the greenery is colouring up and is more lush."

He suddenly spotted the nymph. Hera introduced them to one another. He bent down and shook hands. Then the nymph vanished.

Hera explained about sending out aid to the child, who had sent out the plea for help.

When she had finished speaking, Zeus replied. "Nature's waking up. There will be water spirits appearing next. Everything that we had in the old days when people needed us is happening again."

THE WILDFORESTS OF GREECE

As she positioned herself behind a group of trees, Mia kicked out at one of the tree trunks. In a fierce whisper, she blubbered. "Talk to me as you once did. What's the matter with you?"

The tree stayed silent and listless. She leant against it, almost willing the spirit of the tree that dwelt within to waken up.

The Huntresses were practising stealth and concealment, while Ruby Cameron was putting Anthony Kibble through his newfound Hunter skills. Mia let the thought of Anthony calm and refocus her.

Yes, she was jealous of the long periods of time he spent with Ruby and the gall she had felt when she was passed up to be Artemis's head huntress. Instead, Ruby Cameron had secured the position.

Therefore, feeling resentment and a blazing white-hot bitterness, Mia coolly scanned the terrain. She spotted sudden movement amongst nearby foliage, she tensed, the bush shook again. Mia sprung towards it and peered into leafy darkness.

She was suddenly bowled over by Anthony Kibble, who landed on top of her. Girlish laughter came from the offending bush. Ruby and Sofia emerged, covered in twigs and leaves.

Anthony grinned down at her; Mia relaxed and battered her eyelashes at him in mock flirtation. She also started to laugh. She held on to him a couple of moments longer than necessary.

Anthony climbed back onto his feet and offered Mia his hand. She took it and he pulled her to her feet.

"If that's with your new hunter skills, I'm not impressed." She mockingly commented. Anthony pretended to look hurt.

Mia waved to Ruby and strode off to hide herself in the foliage once again. Ruby's jaw muscles tightened. No one had ever flouted or undermined her authority quite like Mia and Mia knew exactly where to stick it. In addition, she was vying for Anthony's affections. After concealment practise, Ruby was going to call for sword sparring.

"How about if I make Mia my sparring partner?" Ruby thought with grim satisfaction. Anthony must have picked up on her thought pattern because he murmured into her ear.

"That's not the way to handle her. Let me knock some of the cockiness out of her."

"She's got years of experience behind her. At least you're immortal so we won't be scooping you up off the ground," she mouthed.

"Never forget that I'm the son of Apollo, I bet my dad was a dab hand with a sword as well as the bow and arrow." Ruby thought on it. Anthony's suggestion had merit behind it.

"All right then, she's got a swift lunge. So watch out for it."

"Thanks, she'll be less cocky with you afterwards. I guarantee it."

An hour later, Ruby called for sparring practise, there were a few protests about feeling tired and wanting to sleep, but Sofia rallied them together. The girls responded to Sofia more so than they did to Ruby. Anthony started to take note to how they reacted when Ruby issued orders.

The Huntresses were his aunt's army. If they had sworn to be his protectors and to watch over him as an infant, it had taken total dedication to their future leader. He needed to gain their loyalty and trust. Ruby was good at her job, but Anthony also noted, she hadn't got any people skills.

He had to do something about that. Otherwise, the huntresses would fall apart and Anthony Kibble did not want to hear the ire of his aunt's tongue.

Everyone started issuing challenges to one another. Ruby was on the verge of calling Mia forward, she had dismissed her earlier conversation with Anthony entirely.

Anthony unsheathed his sword and shouted "Mia, to me." Mia spun around, her sword flashing radiant reflection from the sun.

"Are you sure?" She asked

Anthony's face suddenly hardened into a stony mask, and when he spoke, his voice sounded lyrical.

"Give me the best you've got." She was on him then, all feline grace with deadly intent.

She thrust with her sword (just as Ruby had warned him about). He easily parried it and followed up with a few slashes of his own. Mia fell back into a defensive stance, warding off Anthony's blows and waiting for him to make the first mistake.

They both stood their ground, trading ripostes, neither one backing down. Ruby was also raining blows on Sofia, but both girls stopped to watch Anthony. His face betrayed no emotion. Mia was good, he could tell. A voice inside his mind told him, "I'm better."

Mia grinned at him and in that moment, he broke through her parry and lunged. She jumped back and brought her sword around to block. The rest of the huntresses had stopped fencing and was watching the main event unfold.

Some of them were cheering "Mia, Mia." Anthony smiled inwardly. "Now." He thought he heard Apollo speaking to him.

"Son, knock her block off." His dad was having a good time at his expense and Anthony loved it.

"Anthony, rally my girls to you. They'll listen." His aunt and his dad were watching him beat Mia to a pulp. He managed a sword pommel strike, which caught Mia unawares and nearly knocked her out. Ruby, Sofia and the rest of the Huntresses all chanted in unison. "Anthony, Anthony."

The tide had changed in his favour. He brought his sword sweeping towards his opponent's legs. Mia stumbled backwards and fell to meet earth.

The camp was ecstatic. All the girls ran towards Anthony, slapping him on the back, shaking his hand and best of all, Ruby giving him a slow, passionate and lingering kiss. Then she blushed at her own daring.

"That was the first time I've ever been beaten." Mia came forward, holding her ribs and grinning.

"Yes, well, I am the esteemed true leader." The girls froze at Anthony's pronouncement and suddenly, like rivers merging into the sea, they converged as one, pledging their loyalty as they once did eons ago.

REALM OF HADES

The river Styx gurgled nosily in the gloom and echoed around the inner sanctum of Hades' chamber. Pearlescent red glowed off the walls from the flickering flames hanging from their brackets.

Hades coolly pondered over the fresh news that his spy had revealed about Anthony Kibble and Artemis's Huntresses. It was time to turn on the heat. Hades knew all about Ruby Cameron. The only way to cripple Anthony was to attack his favourite girl and it would be priceless just to see the expression on Anthony's face when he found out about Ruby's past.

Homer had deceived him and had sided with Anthony, then he had moved on into the afterlife once he had broken the shackles Hades had placed on him millennia ago.

THE WILDFORESTS OF GREECE

The night was hushed, not a breath of wind rustled the trees and the pale moon shone its silvery glow into Ruby Cameron's tent. The soft beams highlighted her still form.

Selene the moon goddess smiled as she glided across the sky, she knew about Ruby's affections towards Anthony Kibble and the trials Ruby still had to face before her fate entwined with Anthony's on a lasting basis. It was preordained by the fates that they were meant to be romantically involved. The son of Apollo and Aphrodite (the perfect male and female) destined to find love with the purest of Artemis's huntresses. The deities knew this to be gospel eons ago and it still held sway even now.

Artemis herself had purposely handpicked Ruby by her loyalty to the hunt and her devotion to willingly serve and pledge her life to heal others.

Something had happened in the past that had stopped Ruby's spiritual progress and her ability to heal had dried up.

Selene lingered to send silver wisps of dreams into Ruby's tent.

The bloodstone felt too heavy on the young girl's finger, her shoulder length flaming red hair sparkled with electricity as she placed her small hand over the fallen soldier.

Her name was Ruby Cameron and she was 8 years old. She was too young to be in the middle of a war zone, but she had insisted that the immortal Huntress Artemis would watch and protect her. Since her parents were proud that Ruby had decided to dedicate her life as a follower of the goddess of the hunt, they had agreed to let her enter the battle-scarred landscape.

Now she was administering her healing through the bloodstone that she carried on her finger as a ring. The soldier moved feebly and moaned. "You're going to be all right." Ruby soothed.

"Of course he will be."

Ruby looked up and her eyes flashed at the sudden voice that had disturbed the healing vibrations. A girl, roughly around Ruby's age, had sauntered over. She smiled warmly.

"I'm Mia. I too am a follower of the immortal Artemis. Goddess of the hunt."

"Ruby Cameron," Ruby said. She kept her voice low and firm. No one had dared to interrupt her while she was acting as a conduit of energy before. This girl needed to be taught her place. Ruby felt as if an immortal hand was touching her shoulder, sustaining her from being too rash. Ruby automatically knew it was Artemis chiding her.

"I was in the middle of something." Ruby admitted with a small smile. Mia laughed.

"I like you. I guess we'll be close friends at some point."

"I like that very much." Ruby shook hands.

The dream faded and a new morning dawned fetching a faint drizzle of rain and a breeze. Ruby awoke feeling restful and wondering why she had been dreaming about her past friendship with Mia.

ANTHONY KIBBLE

Anthony awoke, feeling achy and sore from his fencing match with Mia. Somehow he knew that since he had won the Huntresses allegiance and had taken over the chain of command from Ruby, that the balance had shifted.

But, he mused, how to properly train and motivate them when he, himself, had no military academia. He had no proper ranking.

"Follow your instincts, my son." Apollo spoke inside Anthony's head. Golden light glowed inside the tent and Apollo materialized before Anthony's eyes.

"Don't worry about mundane matters such as material titles and rank. You are pure god now. Homer helped you, didn't he?"

"Yes, he did. But I don't know how to be a leader."

"I cannot help you decide what to do. I will only say this. Get the one person who has never been given a chance to prove herself, on your side."

Anthony instantly thought of Mia, it suddenly dawned on him that she felt bitter and angry towards Ruby, because Ruby had usurped the position of leader of the Huntresses, and really it was Mia who was the rightful head.

"I never knew that it was Mia that I was meant to help." Anthony said.

Apollo smiled, "Ruby Cameron won't take it lightly. When it comes to challenging her authority, even your aunt has her hands full."

Anthony grinned. "I'll bet."

"Just one other piece of advice before I leave. Stay the course." Apollo dissipated and Anthony knew in his heart of hearts just what he had to do.

THE LOST HOPES OF THE RIVER STYX

The wailing despairing voices gurgled and sobbed as the Styx flowed through the underworld. "Hera, queen of the gods. Why have you forsaken us when we needed you the most?" The lost souls cried in anguish.

Their phantom dull grey forms, that used to glow silver, were on the verge of turning black as they aimlessly swam the never-ending swim of night.

PENDLE HILL

The nymph of Pendle that the gods and goddesses had awakened from his dormant slumber, suddenly shrieked as if he had been burnt. He clasped his gnarl like hands to his head.

"What is it?" exclaimed Hera in alarm (the goddesses had just finished band practise. The Band of the Immortals was coming on strong).

"Voices calling for help, from a place called Styx." Sobbed the nymph.

Hera blanched. "Styx. You're hearing the lost souls of our Underworld?"

"Yes. I can hear them calling out to you for help."

Hera looked at her friends. It was Athena that voiced all their concerns.

"Who silenced the lost souls? Because that's why we left Olympus in the first place. No one was praying to us anymore."

After a silent unspoken moment, Aphrodite glanced between Hera and the nymph, "How come the voices are praying just to her?"

"I'm thinking that myself." Athena chimed in.

Hera clenched her hands into fists. She suddenly felt like slapping Aphrodite's face, but settled for saying, "I really don't know why me."

"Well, isn't it obvious that you are favoured by the Lost Souls, darling." Aphrodite said acidly.

Just at that moment, Apollo arrived on the scene. "The nymph of Pendle has just been and informed me that scorn and envy has crept back amongst us once again."

"So, what if it has?" Aphrodite challenged him.

Apollo suddenly did something that was not like him at all. He scooped and draped Aphrodite over his shoulder, and bodily carried her away.

Hera and Athena looked on in admiration at Apollo's daring. "Just why did you take Aphrodite's side earlier?" Hera asked.

"You know I'm warlike in nature and in spirit."

"Athena, you know you are a goddess. Don't you?"

The two women burst into fits of nonstop laughter at their own jibes. There was a faint noise like a raspberry being blown and a snickering nymphish laugh coming from inside the hill.

"I've heard you made a spectacle of yourself." Hephaestus commented to Aphrodite. They were inside their cabin. Husband and wife glared at one another.

"Don't start on me." She said coolly. She couldn't keep the honey laced sarcasm from her voice.

IN THE MIST: OVER THE WILDFOREST OF GREECE

Artemis gazed down at Anthony Kibble. She was keeping a watch on his progress as he was interacting with her Huntresses. Of all the goddesses, she was the only one close to nature, she knew all the stones, foliage and how to plan for ambushes.

She could easily get along with Athena. Battle plans and hunting works hand in hand.

Her girls were dotty over Anthony, especially Ruby Cameron! Artemis thought about the prophecy that was proclaimed eons ago. A son of Aphrodite and Apollo finds love with a Huntress of Artemis.

"A Huntress, but not my head Huntress anymore," she thought to herself in regret and determination. Anthony Kibble had his hands full. He needed to get Mia on his side and to give her the rank of head Huntress over Ruby.

That would sting. Ruby would feel betrayed. Artemis knew about the spy among her girls. It was Hades that was influencing Ruby in her dreams and making her think she had fallen for him.

He had her spy for him and report on Anthony's progress. That was why the goddesses had to contain the leak.

Artemis knew just by doing some spying on her own and by what Aphrodite had confided when she left Anthony in the Sanctuary of Healing in Ruby's care.

And it would wound Anthony to the core, like it did for Hercules eons ago!

RIVER STYX

The waters gurgled as Hades stretched out his hand one last time; he needed an ace in the hole. One last card to play! Artemis had overplayed her hand by snooping around. Ruby Cameron had informed him and now Ruby felt ashamed of not being perfect by betraying her esteemed leader.

Hades knew that only one person would really steam the goddess of the hunt. Her ongoing feud with Pandora.

Hence, he was calling Pandora to rise out of the river Styx. She obeyed, she rose out of the water still clutching her box and her blonde tresses were sopping wet.

Her very first words were "Where is Artemis right now?"

"All in good time."

"Don't give me that. Just point me in the right direction."

She strode off when Hades pointed to the right passageway out of his realm.

About the Author

"A Change of Views" was written by Craig Hartley, pictured above.

Craig started writing poems from the age of 14, with his first inspiration leading him to write the poem entitled "Troubles of A Boy". Now aged 44, Craig is an accomplished writer of over 100 poems and continues his writing to this day.

Craig happens to have Down's syndrome but this will never deter him from living a life of his own choosing and he is clear that it does not define him. Craig's poem entitled "One Man's Struggle" depicts his utter determination to fulfil his personal ambitions.

Craig has performed his poems in speech and drama classes, in local theatres and libraries across Lancashire, which has gained him local celebrity status over the years.

Craig has achieved many goals during his life. He achieved NVQs, including Business Administration; GCSES, including English Grade C and has qualifications in Creative Writing and Desktop Publishing. When he finished college, Craig was keen to be employed. He has worked for

Lancashire Constabulary, Burnley Youth Theatre and more recently Community Solutions as an invaluable member of their administration team. He is a self-confessed perfectionist, who loves to read, watch films, listen to music and is driven to succeed in his various escapades.

One of his main passions is dance. Craig is a successful dancer, having completed several exams and won many competitions for tap, ballroom, old time and Latin American dancing. He is an avid supporter of DanceSyndrome, a Lancashire based inclusive dance charity.

Craig has previously been successful in fundraising for DanceSyndrome through the sale of a book of his favourite poems. He is also donating all proceeds from the sale of this book to the charity.

DanceSyndrome was the inspiration of founder, Jen Blackwell, who also has Down's syndrome. She wanted to follow her dream of being a dancer and dance leader. Jen had a firm belief that 'anything is possible even if you have a learning disability'. DanceSyndrome was established in 2009 and that concept is the foundation for everything that the charity does.

DanceSyndrome has an equal number of learning disabled and non-disabled company members and provides inclusive dance and leadership opportunities for anyone who believes disability should not be a barrier to living life to the full.

All dance activity is led and informed by people with learning disabilities. DanceSyndrome activities give people a healthy life-style – and much more. Their work promotes confidence, respect, self-belief and social inclusion through a philosophy of focusing on ability instead of disability.

Their vision for the future is simple. They want to empower learning disabled individuals through inclusive dance activities. For more information visit www.dancesyndrome.co.uk

Printed in Great Britain
by Amazon

50639676R00035